Rabbids Invasion

Attack of the Zombie Rabbids

Adapted by Maggie Testa
Based on the screenplay written by Mélanie Duval
Illustrated by Shane L. Johnson

Ready-to-Read

Simon Spotlight
New York   London   Toronto   Sydney   New Delhi

SIMON SPOTLIGHT
An imprint of Simon & Schuster Children's Publishing Division
1230 Avenue of the Americas, New York, New York 10020
This Simon Spotlight edition July 2016

SIMON SPOTLIGHT, READY-TO-READ, and colophon are registered trademarks of Simon & Schuster, Inc.
For information about special discounts for bulk purchases, please contact Simon & Schuster Special Sales at
1-866-506-1949 or business@simonandschuster.com.
Manufactured in the United States of America 0616 LAK
2 4 6 8 10 9 7 5 3 1
ISBN 978-1-4814-6067-5 (hc)
ISBN 978-1-4814-6066-8 (pbk)
ISBN 978-1-4814-6068-2 (eBook)

CONTENTS

CHAPTER 1:
Delicious-Looking Round Things

It was a quiet day at the mall. A Rabbid was strolling along cleaning his armpits with an armpit brush (also known as a toothbrush, but the Rabbid didn't know that). As he wandered down the hallway, something caught his attention.

It was a group of three Rabbids. One
of them was wearing a cereal box on his
head. One of them was just standing there.
And one of them was holding something.

The something was round. The something had a hole in the center. The something looked delicious.

The Rabbid licked his lips. He had to have it.

The Rabbid walked over, ready
for a trade. He offered his shiny, red
armpit brush in exchange for the
delicious-looking round thing (also known
as a doughnut, but the Rabbid didn't know
that). The other Rabbids looked at their
box filled with doughnuts, and then they
looked at the armpit brush. One of the
Rabbids walked over with the treat.

It looked like he was going to make the trade. The first Rabbid handed over his armpit brush. He couldn't wait to try the delicious-looking round thing. But just as the other Rabbid was about to hand it over, he shoved it in his mouth instead!

"BWAHAHAHAHA!"

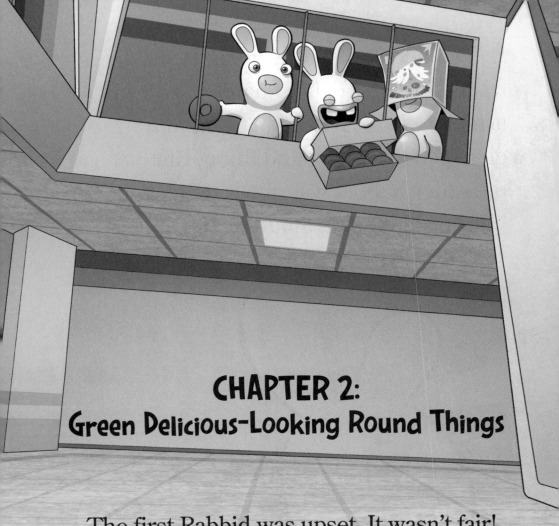

CHAPTER 2:
Green Delicious-Looking Round Things

The first Rabbid was upset. It wasn't fair! He hung his head in sorrow as he rode down the escalator. In response the other Rabbids threw the armpit brush at his head. *Thwack!* He looked up at the group of Rabbids who were taunting him from above. This meant that he wasn't looking when he

reached the end of the escalator. *Plonk!* He tripped and fell facedown on the floor.

"BWAHAHAHAHA!" laughed the other Rabbids.

The Rabbid shook his fist in the direction of the mean Rabbids. Then he stormed away. But all was not lost. He soon came across something very interesting. It was another box filled with delicious-looking round things. They even looked more delicious than the ones in the last box because this time they were green! Things were looking up!

The Rabbid ran over and tossed one in his mouth before any other Rabbids could come by and steal them from him. He thought he'd feel great, just like the other Rabbids did, but instead he doubled over in pain. What was happening?

Just then two other Rabbids walked by. One of them poked him with the leek he was holding (because why wouldn't he be holding a leek?). At first the Rabbid didn't respond, so the other Rabbid kept poking. Then he turned around.

The Rabbid groaned. He shuffled across the floor. He had turned green, just like the green delicious-looking round thing he had eaten! He had turned into a Zombie Rabbid!

Chapter 3:
Escape from the Zombie Rabbid!

The other two Rabbids screamed and ran away to hide, because, well, who wouldn't hide from a Zombie Rabbid? But from their hiding place, they noticed something. . . it was the Zombie Rabbid's box filled with green delicious-looking round things!

They didn't know that it was these same doughnuts that had caused the first Rabbid to turn into a zombie. And so they definitely didn't know that these doughnuts would do the same thing to them. All they knew was that they had to feast on them right away. They just had to get past the scary green Zombie Rabbid first. It was worth the risk.

The Rabbids ducked down. They jumped. They slid on their bellies. But it was actually pretty easy to get around the Zombie Rabbid. Zombies are very slow, after all. But then, just as the Rabbids were about to dig in, the Zombie Rabbid turned around and started shuffling back toward them!

The Rabbids screamed! They had to get themselves—and the green delicious-looking round things— somewhere safe!

The Rabbids grabbed the box and ran to the escalator. They thought they could make a quick getaway, but of course they chose the down escalator instead of the one going up. They struggled and went nowhere until a woman with a cart ran into

them. She was so interested in her phone that she didn't even notice the two Rabbids that had joined her for the ride. The Rabbids came right back down and were face-to-face with the Zombie Rabbid— again! This was not good.

There was only one thing left to do!
Whack! Whack! They started throwing
their precious green doughnuts at the
Zombie Rabbid. But he just kept coming!
"BWAHAHAHAHA!" the Rabbids cried.
They ran into the elevator now, and this time
they managed to get to the second floor.
Could they finally eat the rest of their green
delicious-looking round things in peace?

No! When they got to the second floor,
they saw something else they didn't
like . . . other Rabbids. They weren't Zombie
Rabbids, but they would certainly try to
steal their green delicious-looking round
things. Rabbids like delicious-looking food,
you see. The Rabbids went right back down.

As you probably could have guessed, when the elevator door opened, there was a deep "raaaah!" There was the Zombie Rabbid again! He groaned and shuffled right over to the two Rabbids!

The Rabbids ran as fast as they could away from him, right into a photo booth. They closed the curtain. But were they finally safe? They shivered in fear and hugged one another as they waited in silence for the Zombie Rabbid to walk by.

When they didn't hear the Zombie
Rabbid anymore, one of the Rabbids
peeked out his head from behind the
curtain to check that the coast was clear.
But he only checked one direction! The
two Rabbids ran out of the photo booth and
straight into the Zombie Rabbid!

Panicking, the Rabbids ran the other way until they came to a dead end made of boxes. (Or at least they thought it was a dead end. The Rabbids didn't check to see if they could go around.)

The Zombie Rabbid was closing in. What would they do? One of the Rabbids tried running into the dead end to knock it over. He only managed to nearly knock himself out. Then the other Rabbid climbed up the boxes. "BWAHAHAHAHA!" he laughed at his partner below. He was about to leave his partner in the dust when the other Rabbid hopped up too. Then they both jumped off and continued running.

CHAPTER 4:
Snack Time!

The Rabbids were still looking for a place to hide from the Zombie Rabbid and enjoy their treats when they came across a large machine. It was one of those machines that had lots of snacks inside. So what did Rabbids do? Did they keep running to stay safe? Of course not! They stopped and tried to get some snacks out of the machine. And as usually occurs when Rabbids put their heads in vending machines, one of them got stuck. The other pulled and pulled, but the Rabbid wouldn't budge.

Thankfully, they had help. Another mysterious Rabbid caught up to them and helped them pull. *Pop!* The Rabbid was free!

The Rabbids went to thank whoever
had helped them. "Bwah, bwah bwah,"
the Rabbid said, extending his arm for a
handshake. But oh no! It wasn't just any
Rabbid helping them. It was the Zombie
Rabbid!

The two Rabbids ran away screaming...
again. On their way they dropped one
of the doughnuts in front of the group of
three Rabbids. One was still wearing a
cereal box on his head. The three Rabbids
licked their lips and closed in on the treat.
What do you think happened to those
Rabbids? We'll find out soon.

Meanwhile, the two Rabbids had found the perfect hiding place. It was cool. It was bright. It had a door to keep the Zombie Rabbid out. They were finally safe to eat some green delicious-looking round things.

One of the Rabbids bit into one. And then . . .

He turned into another Zombie Rabbid!
The other Rabbid grabbed the rest of the
green delicious-looking round things and
bolted out of the hiding place. Now he
was alone against two Zombie Rabbids!
He dove under a shelf. Surely the Zombie
Rabbids couldn't get to him here.

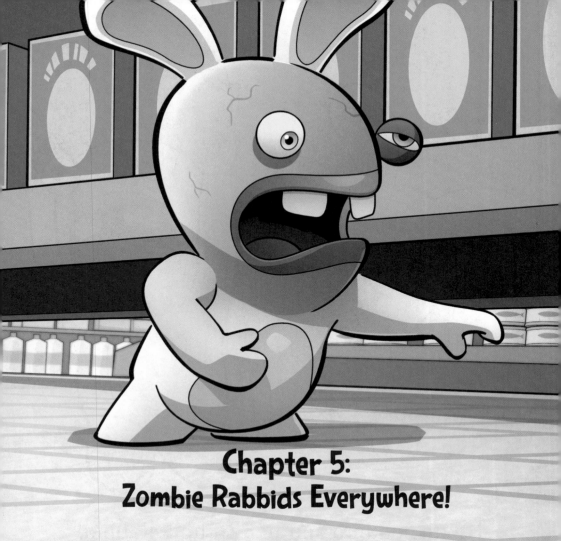

Chapter 5:
Zombie Rabbids Everywhere!

And his plan would have worked . . . had he been quiet. But the Rabbid couldn't resist eating what he found on the floor underneath the shelf—a deliciously tasty stale pretzel.

Crunch!

The Zombie Rabbids followed the noise. They closed in on our dear Rabbid. He had no choice but to run away . . . again!

But everywhere the Rabbid turned, there were more and more Zombie Rabbids coming for him! The group of three now-Zombie Rabbids shuffled over

The Rabbid had no other choice but to run outside, away from the mall.

He finally stopped running when he found a nice trash bin to hide behind. It smelled disgusting, but the Rabbid liked it!

CHAPTER 6:
You Are What You Eat

The Rabbid looked down at the box he was holding. There was one green delicious-looking round thing left. He was the luckiest Rabbid in the world. But not quite yet—the Zombie Rabbids were still coming!

There was only one more place where the Rabbid could go. He could escape by climbing on top of the trash bin. The Zombie Rabbids surrounded the trash bin, but they couldn't reach him. Zombie Rabbids can't jump, you see.

Finally the Rabbid could take his long-awaited bite. He opened his mouth wide and chomped down.

Oh no.